I0703416

The Legend
of the
Rainbow Unicorn

A BEDTIME STORY FROM

THE REALMS BEYOND THE RAINBOW

※　　※　　※　　※

C. S. Johnson

<u>THE LEGEND OF THE RAINBOW UNICORN: OR, HOW THE HORSE BECAME A UNICORN</u>

Copyright © 2022 by C. S. Johnson

1st Edition

ISBN ebook: 978-1-948464-78-9

ISBN hardback: 978-1-94864-79-6

**THIS STORY IS NOT MEANT TO BE HERETICAL. THIS IS NOT A FAITHFUL ADAPTATION OF THE GENESIS ACCOUNT FOUND IN THE BIBLE. THE BIBLE IS THE INERRANT WORD OF GOD.
THIS STORY IS NOT.**

This story is part of THE REALMS BEYOND THE RAINBOW, a Christian fantasy romance series from C. S. Johnson.

THIS BOOK IS DEDICATED TO MY KO-FI SUPPORTERS

I don't know all of you in real life, but the idea that someone would believe in me enough to give me money is just a miracle. Thank you for being one of my miracles.

Leslie Z.
Good-N-Crazy
Natalie N.
Evan P.
Laura A. Grace, Manga Lover, Author
Janice R.
Christina M., New Author
Amy M.
Ani S.
Karen L.
Joshua E.
Timothy W.
Esther K.
David W.
Chris S.
Beth C.
Marty H.
Generic Entity
Stephen Dawkins
Jacob Airey of StudioJake, Author
J. Riley Castine, Author
Bryn Shutt, Author
Donna S.
Jeremy R.
Terri Rand, Future Author
Melinda M.

Listen to my books for free when you subscribe to my YouTube Channel:
https://www.youtube.com/c/writercsjohnson

Find the first chapter of *Kitsunkeo* here:
https://www.youtube.com/watch?v=wf4vqsNMyEY

Also, be the first to see what's coming next when you support me on Ko-Fi!

<u>https://www.ko-fi.com/writercsjohnson</u>

6

LIGHT...
ANIMALS...
MAN...

GOD HAD MAN NAME ALL THE ANIMALS.
BUT THERE WAS STILL NO COMPANION JUST RIGHT FOR MAN.
SO MAN FELL ASLEEP, AND GOD TOOK A RIB FROM HIS SIDE...
...AND GOD MADE WOMAN.

AND BEFORE HE FELL INTO SIN, SO MAN FELL IN LOVE.
THIS IS NOW BONE OF MY BONES AND FLESH OF MY FLESH.

MAN THEN TOOK WOMAN TO MEET THE ANIMALS.
ALL ANIMALS APPROACHED EAGERLY, BUT THE HORSE CAME FORWARD AND REVERENTLY OFFERED TO CARRY WOMAN AS SHE MET THE OTHERS.
FOR HIS KIND SERVICE AND HUMBLE HEART, MAN ASKED GOD TO GIVE THE HORSE A GIFT.

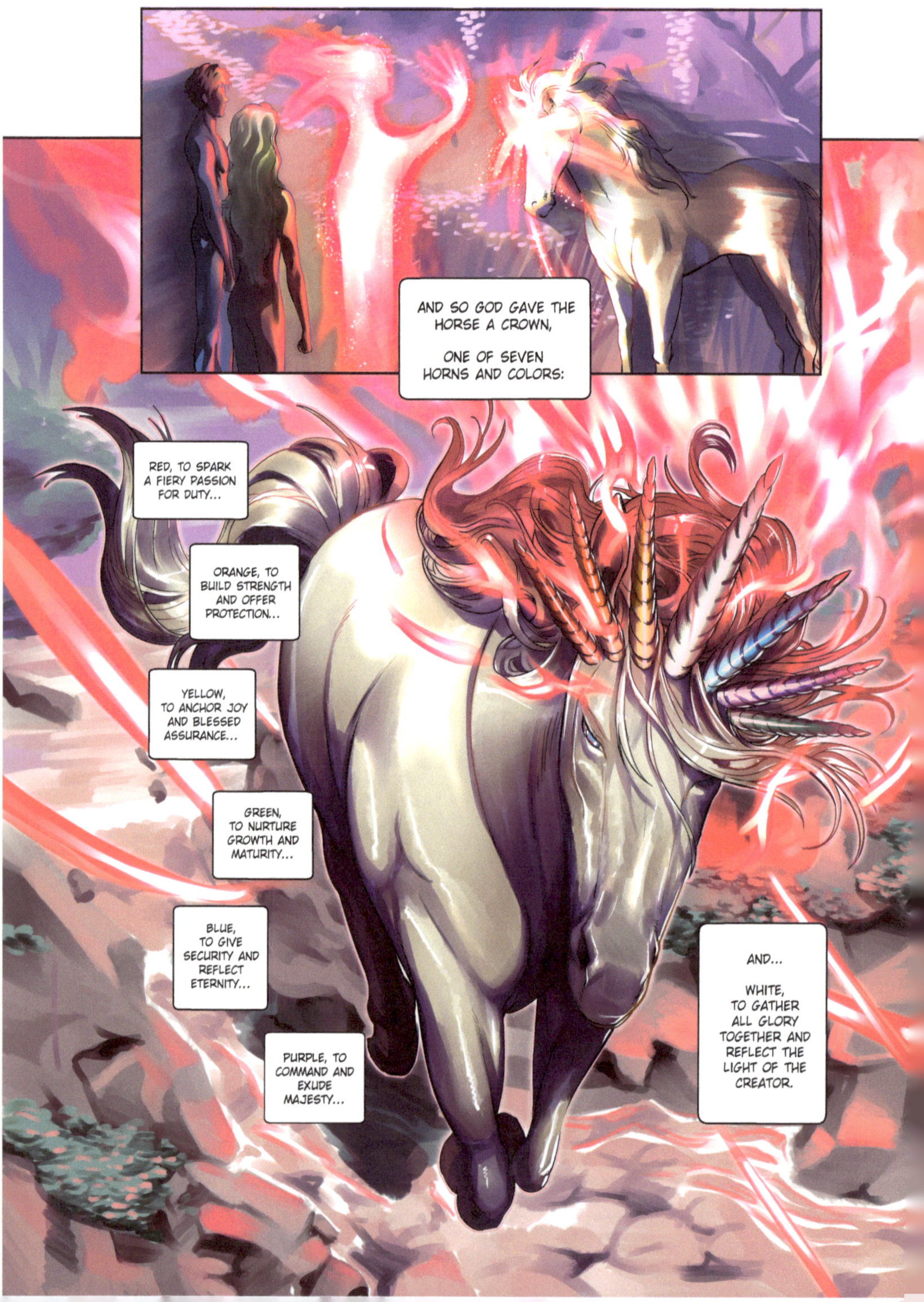

AND SO GOD GAVE THE HORSE A CROWN,

ONE OF SEVEN HORNS AND COLORS:

RED, TO SPARK A FIERY PASSION FOR DUTY...

ORANGE, TO BUILD STRENGTH AND OFFER PROTECTION...

YELLOW, TO ANCHOR JOY AND BLESSED ASSURANCE...

GREEN, TO NURTURE GROWTH AND MATURITY...

BLUE, TO GIVE SECURITY AND REFLECT ETERNITY...

PURPLE, TO COMMAND AND EXUDE MAJESTY...

AND...

WHITE, TO GATHER ALL GLORY TOGETHER AND REFLECT THE LIGHT OF THE CREATOR.

AND GOD SAID, "WHOEVER WISHES TO BE GREAT AMONG YOU WILL BE YOUR SERVANT."
AND THINGS WERE VERY GOOD.

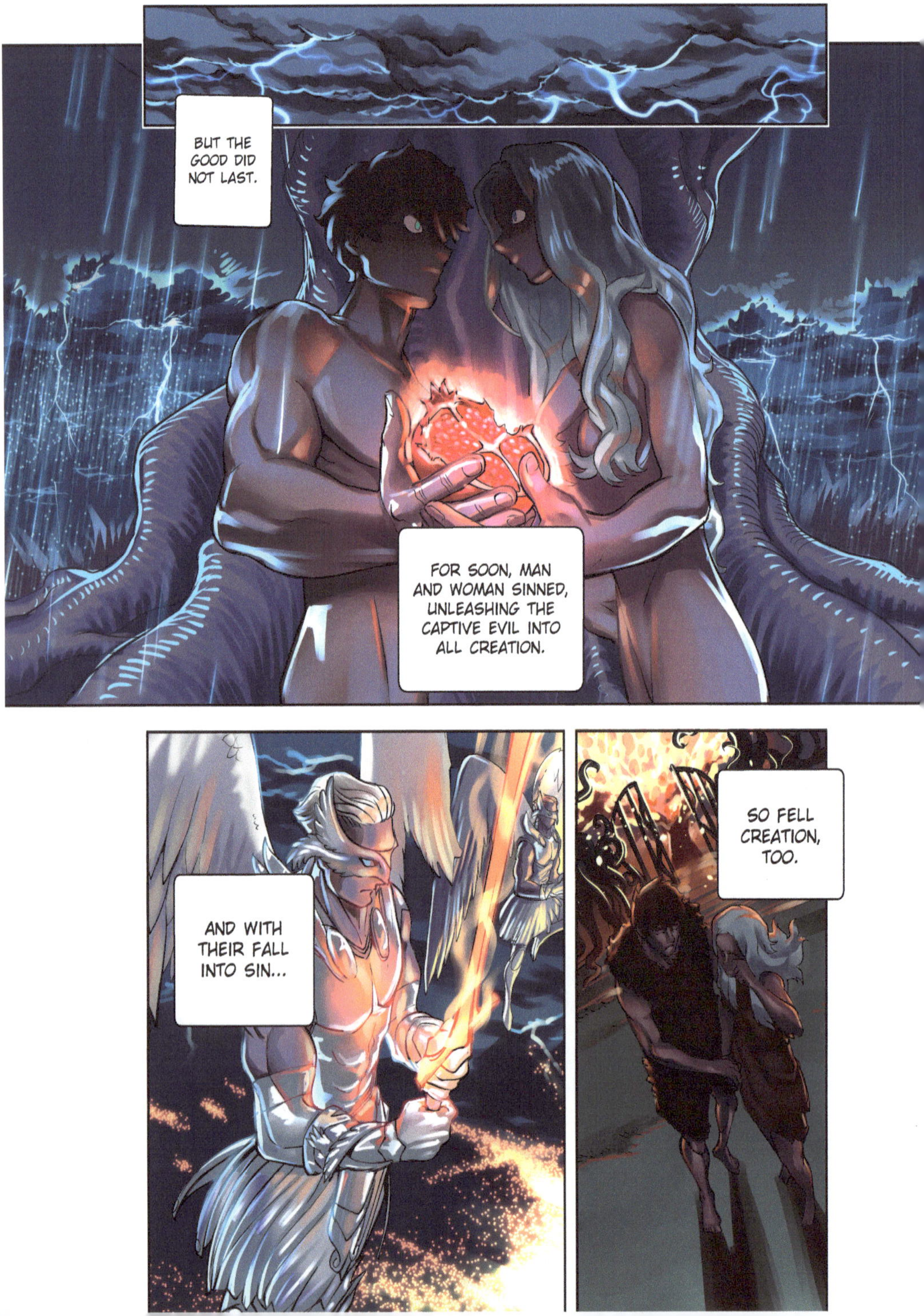

BUT THE GOOD DID NOT LAST.

FOR SOON, MAN AND WOMAN SINNED, UNLEASHING THE CAPTIVE EVIL INTO ALL CREATION.

AND WITH THEIR FALL INTO SIN...

SO FELL CREATION, TOO.

MAN AND WOMAN, NOW CALLED ADAM AND EVE, STRUGGLED TO MAKE A HOME CUT OFF FROM GOD.
BUT THE CROWNED HORSE REMEMBERED GOD, AND FOUND HIMSELF A HOME WITH ABEL, THE FAITHFUL SON OF ADAM.
ABEL LOVED THE CROWNED HORSE AND GAVE HIM A NAME: KLEON.

AND WHEN ABEL WAS MURDERED BY HIS BROTHER CAIN...
HIS BLOOD CRIED OUT AS IT SPILLED OVER THE GROUND.
IT WAS THEN THAT KLEON VOWED TO PROTECT ABEL'S FAMILY.
WHEN GOD DECIDED TO FLOOD THE WORLD WITH WATER, KLEON WAS DETERMINED TO SAVE ABEL'S FAMILY FROM THE GREAT FLOOD.
ABEL'S WIFE AGREED TO KLEON'S PLAN, BUT NEITHER OF THEM ASKED GOD FOR HIS BLESSING -- OR HIS PERMISSION.

USING THE POWER IN HIS CROWN, KLEON OPENED THE RAINBOW PORTAL, INTO THE WORLD NOW KNOWN AS TOULACOEUR.
KLEON WAS THE GUARDIAN OF ABEL'S WIFE AND CHILDREN. TOGETHER THEY MOVED INTO THE NEW REALM WITH OTHER CREATURES AND ANIMALS WHO WERE LOYAL TO ABEL'S LEGACY.
THERE WERE THE DRAGONS, FEARSOME BEASTS OF POWER AND FIRE...
THERE WERE THE ELVES, DISTRIBUTING BEAUTY AND CARE THROUGHOUT THE LAND...
THERE WERE THE GRIFFINS, CUNNING ANIMALS CAPABLE OF GREAT ENDURANCE...
THERE WERE CHANGELINGS, PLAYFUL CREATURES WHO LOVED LAUGHTER...
THERE WERE THE MERMAIDS, GIFTED WITH SONG AS THEY NAVIGATED SEAS...
THERE WERE THE GROUNDLINGS, DETERMINED DIGGERS WHO SOUGHT BEAUTY...
ALL OF THESE CREATIONS CAME TO SERVE ABEL'S FAMILY IN THE NEW REALM. ONCE THE PORTAL CLOSED, THE PEOPLE SETTLED IN.

TIME PASSED, AND SIN ONCE MORE SEEPED INTO THE LAND. THROUGHOUT THE WORLD, THE HUMANS FORGOT GOD AND BEGAN TO SEEK POWER.
AND SO, THEIR STRIFE BEGAN AGAIN.
ABEL'S FIRSTBORN, WHO TENDED TO THE DRAGONS, SOON DEMANDED TO BE MADE KING OF TOULACOEUR.
BUT KLEON REFUSED, VOWING TO SERVE ONLY UNDER ABEL'S WIFE.
SENSING DANGER, EACH OF ABEL'S OTHER CHILDREN TOOK CONTROL OF THE OTHER POWERFUL CREATURES, AND USED THEM TO ESTABLISH THEIR OWN KINGDOMS.
AS THEY EACH GREW MORE POWERFUL, THE REALM FRACTURED, AND THEIR FAMILIES DRIFTED APART.
AND THEN, TRAGICALLY, ABEL'S FIRSTBORN USED HIS DRAGONS TO ATTACK KLEON AND TORE THE RED HORN FROM HIS CROWN.
AFTER THE ATTACK, KLEON MADE A VOW HE WOULD ONLY ANSWER TO WOMAN, IN THE TRADITION OF SERVING EVE.
ABEL'S OTHER OFFSPRING GREW RESTLESS. SENSING KLEON'S WEAKNESS, THEY DEMANDED PROTECTION FROM THE DRAGON CLAN.
DEFEATED AND DISCOURAGED, KLEON RELUCTANTLY RELENTED.

TO KEEP THE REALM FROM DESTRUCTION, KLEON FURTHER BROKE HIS OWN CROWN:

THE ORANGE HORN WENT TO THE GRIFFIN KEEPERS, AND IT WAS PASSED DOWN ALONG THE GENERATIONS.

THE YELLOW HORN WAS GIVEN TO THE GROUNDLINGS, AND IT WAS LOST AMONG THE TREASURES THEY BROUGHT FORTH FROM THE EARTH;

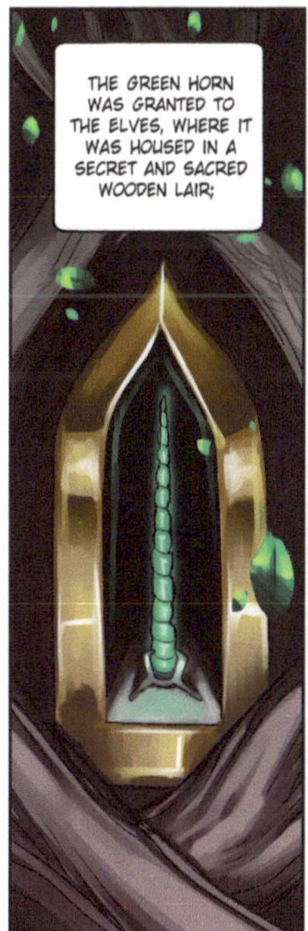

THE GREEN HORN WAS GRANTED TO THE ELVES, WHERE IT WAS HOUSED IN A SECRET AND SACRED WOODEN LAIR;

THE BLUE HORN WAS GIFTED TO THE MERMAIDS, WHO BOUND IT INSIDE THE HEART OF THE SEA;

THE PURPLE HORN WAS PASSED TO THE CHANGELINGS, WHO CHANGED IT COMPLETELY, MAKING IT AND THEMSELVES UNRECOGNIZABLE.

KLEON KEPT THE WHITE HORN, KEEPING WATCH OVER TOULACOEUR.

CENTURIES PASSED, FULL OF DARKNESS AND WAR, OF BUILDING AND BLOOMING, OF TRIALS AND TRIUMPHS...
AND NOW KLEON WAITS AND WATCHES OVER HIS FRACTURED REALM, WITH ONLY A SINGLE HORN ON HIS HEAD, DREAMING OF THE DAY THE REALMS WILL REMEMBER GOD AND BE REUNITED AS ONE...
...BEFORE THEIR SIN AND DEPRAVITY BRING ABOUT THE COMPLETE AND UTTER DESTRUCTION OF LIFE ON THIS SIDE OF THE RAINBOW PORTAL.
AND THAT IS THE LEGEND OF THE RAINBOW UNICORN.

AUTHOR'S NOTE

Dear Reader,

Thank you once more for picking up my work and reading it. This time, I have taken great care to see that you can see more of what's in my head while I write. I am very thankful for my lovely artist, Levi Tonin, and I hope you have enjoyed his work as well as mine this time.

I set out to write The Realms Beyond the Rainbow more than a couple of years ago, and I have every hope of finishing it. But in the meantime, this small little side project of bringing one of Toulacoeur's legends to life with artwork as well as words has given me such joy, and added to my anticipation of the series.

Sometimes as I write I find inspiration in my life experiences: The Starlight Chronicles is an ode to many of my high school years, both in good and bad ways; The Divine Space Pirates was inspired by the political turmoil I've witnessed in my young adulthood; The Order of the Crystal Daggers was my own love letter to both fairy tales and history; and Favan & Flew is my testament to true love. For The Realms Beyond the Rainbow and The Alliance of the Dragon Sword, I find more of my inspiration is grounded in my faith. I love getting to tell these stories (even though they are not true) because it helps me to see how wonderful God is and how much I can see Him as I look back upon my life. While my progress on both series is regrettably slow for now, I am eager to see the finished results.

In the Bible, Paul says we see ourselves through a mirror, though darkly. I imagine that imagery is also a good comparison for my writing and my work. My life is but a poor reflection of the grace I've been given, but I am a happy warrior, and I will continue to write on. The universe is full of mirrors, and while my mirror may be crackled and dark, I intend to reflect the divine light as best as I can.

In addition to Levi, I must also thank my supporters, and I would like to thank my husband and children. They are everything I ever wanted, and more. If I truly believe in true love, it is because I experience it every day with them in my life, and I thank God for giving them to me – and I thank him for giving me you as a reader, too.

I hope you will pick up *Kitsuneko* next, if you haven't already, and learn more about Kleon, Toulacoeur, and more!

Until We Meet Again,

C. S. Johnson